OSHIE

OSHIE

Jon Blake

illustrated by

Anuska Allepuz

WALKER
BOOKS

To Carl Dyer,
for all his help and support,
and Jacky Paynter,
for all her patience and dedication
A.A.

This is a work of fiction. Names, characters, places and incidents are either the product of the author's imagination or, if real, used fictitiously. All statements, activities, stunts, descriptions, information and material of any other kind contained herein are included for entertainment purposes only and should not be relied on for accuracy or replicated as they may result in injury.

First published 2011 by Walker Books Ltd
87 Vauxhall Walk, London SE11 5HJ

3

This book has been typeset in StempelSchneidler

Printed in Great Britain by Clays Ltd, St Ives plc

British Library Cataloguing in Publication Data:
a catalogue record for this book is available from the British Library

ISBN 978-1-4063-2417-4

www.walker.co.uk

Contents

The Eyes of Oshie Black

His name was Black and his eyes were the bluest blue in the universe. They were a blue which belonged under the sea or up in the sky, on a brilliant tropical fish or above a heavenly sunrise. Instead they gazed from the face of a ten-year-old boy sitting on the playground wall of Adams Green Primary School.

It was a steady gaze in those bright blue eyes, a gaze which coolly weighed up the frantic game of playground footy the boy was watching. Oshie Black had never seen these boys before, nor the girls who hopscotched nearby.

Jenna Reece *had* to know who he was. "Are you new?" she asked, marching boldly up to him.

Oshie turned his head away and avoided her eyes. He was shy. Jenna liked that.

"No," he replied. "I'm ten."

Jenna got his joke straight away and laughed. A smile crept on to Oshie's face and, just for a second, his startling blue eyes glanced at her. She had nice eyes too, deep brown ones with a twinkle of fun in them. It was as if they'd always known each other.

Just at that moment, the football came flying straight at Oshie. He caught it with sure hands, then flung it up, up, up into

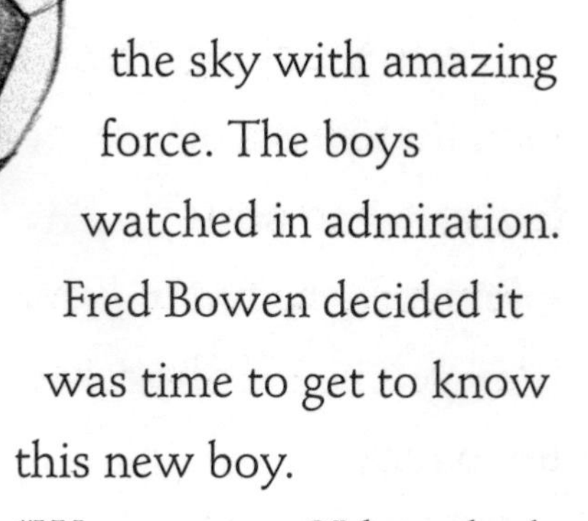

the sky with amazing force. The boys watched in admiration. Fred Bowen decided it was time to get to know this new boy.

"Want a game?" he asked.

A frown came on to Oshie's face. He shook his head.

"Come on!" said Fred. "If you're any good you can play for the school."

Adams Green Primary had a big game coming up – a cup semi-final – and Fred, the captain, was desperate for some more talent.

"Come on!" said the other boys. They'd decided they liked the look of Oshie.

"I'll play," volunteered Jenna.

"It's a boys' game," said Fred.

"It's a boys' game," mocked Jenna, in a silly baby voice.

The boys were still waiting for Oshie. He clambered down from the wall, but as he began to walk towards them it became obvious that something was wrong. Oshie walked with a hobble, his knees tight together, his right foot rising onto his toes and scraping the ground. It was funny, but also scary. Oshie could barely run at all, and as he lunged for the ball he span and dropped onto his backside. Only with difficulty could he turn on to one hand and push himself up again.

At first the boys were transfixed. They stared at Oshie's struggle with the simplest movements, not sure how to react. Should they try to help him?

Should they ignore him? Why had they asked him to play?

It was Fred who'd asked him first, and now he felt stupid, and that made him angry.

"Why do you run like a puppet?" he suddenly asked.

Oshie hobbled round to face Fred. A look as hard as sapphire was in his eyes.

"Why do you talk like a muppet?" he replied.

Fred decided he didn't like this new boy. How dare he call Fred a name when he couldn't even walk properly?

"Just go and sit on your wall," he said.

No one disagreed. The Schools Cup semi-final was coming up fast and they didn't need the likes of Oshie getting in the way.

If Oshie was upset by Fred's comment he didn't show it. Once he was seated in class, equal to everybody else, it didn't take him long to settle in. Miss Rees was first to get the Oshie treatment.

"What came after the Bronze Age?" asked Miss Rees.

Oshie's hand shot up.

"Yes, Osian?" said Miss Rees.

"The Soss Age," replied Oshie.

"That's not a sensible answer, is it, Osian?" said Miss Rees.

"No, miss," replied Oshie.

"Shall we try being sensible?" suggested Miss Rees.

"OK, miss," replied Oshie.

"What came after the Bronze Age?" asked Miss Rees.

"The Cab Age," replied Oshie.

With his shining eyes and cheeky smile, Oshie was

quickly a hit with the girls. Most of the boys were taking to him as well. But after each lesson he'd struggle to his feet, and suddenly he was Oshie the "spaz", Oshie who couldn't play football, Oshie who'd never be part of the gang.

Jenna couldn't stop watching Oshie. It wasn't just that his eyes were so blue and his lashes so long, it was the way he viewed everything – so cool, yet so alert. Oshie never missed a trick. When Miss Rees lost her board marker he knew it was behind the work trays. When Janine started having an asthma attack he was first to try to help.

Jenna had to know more about Oshie. As they collected their coats at the end of the day she sought him out.

"What is wrong with your legs?" asked Jenna.

"Cerebral palsy," answered Oshie. "Want a lychee?"

"What's that?" asked Jenna.

"A fruit," replied Oshie.

"No, cerebral thingy, what is it?"

"Damage in my brain," replied Oshie.

"But you're not stupid," said Jenna.

"It's not that part of my brain," said Oshie.

"Have you always had it?" asked Jenna.

"Yes," replied Oshie. "Want a lychee?"

"OK," said Jenna.

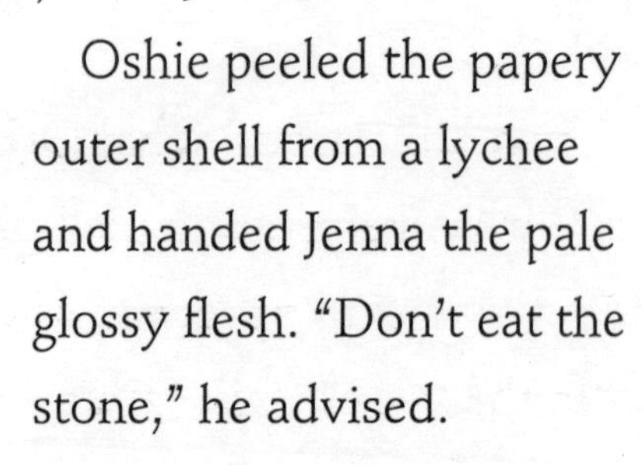

Oshie peeled the papery outer shell from a lychee and handed Jenna the pale glossy flesh. "Don't eat the stone," he advised.

Jenna tasted the lychee. It was sweet, with a perfumed taste, kind of wrong, kind of delicious.

"Why won't the boys let you play football?" asked Oshie.

"I'm too good," replied Jenna.

"How can you be too good?" asked Oshie.

"I always get the ball off them," replied Jenna.

"Ah," said Oshie. "They don't like it."

"They say I cheat," said Jenna. "But I just tackle hard."

Oshie's blue eyes narrowed. He liked Jenna but she was a mouthy type and he didn't know if he could trust what she said. "The boys don't pick the school team," he said.

Jenna understood what Oshie was driving at. "Mr Wilkes doesn't pick me 'cos he doesn't want to upset the boys," she said.

"In that case," said Oshie, "he's an idiot."

"He's useless," replied Jenna. "He only coaches the team 'cos there's no other men teachers."

Oshie looked thoughtful, but whatever he was thinking, he didn't say.

The day of the semi-final drew closer, and the closer it got, the more scared the boys became. Everyone knew Adams Green Primary had been lucky to get so far. They'd had a good draw, played some weak teams and even got a bye in the quarter finals because Gladstone Primary had been closed down before the game. Now, however, they were up against Rushwood Primary, the best team in the local division, unbeaten all year. Rushwood had five players in the county junior team, whereas Adams Green Primary only had Dylan Evans, or David Beckham, as he preferred to be known.

When the big day came, and the team

was announced, they'd just about thought themselves out of any chance of winning. Mr Wilkes didn't help, constantly telling them they'd done well to get this far, and shouldn't be too disappointed if they got hammered. "Life isn't just about winning," Mr Wilkes liked to say.

Oshie had watched all of the practices. No one had asked him to be there, but he sat quietly on the sidelines nibbling his lychees, and Mr Wilkes was too embarrassed to ask him to leave. As the teams ran out for the final he was there again, watching, watching, while Jenna took her usual seat on the bench and prepared for another afternoon's frustration.

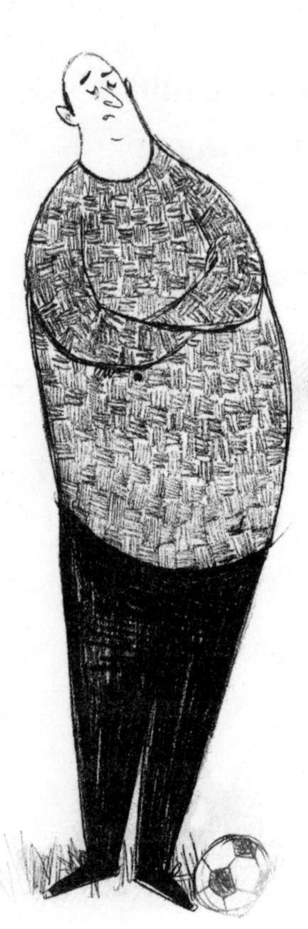

It was all horribly predictable. By half-time Rushwood were three up, and it could have been seven. The team traipsed back to Mr Wilkes, heads down, and although Mr Wilkes told them there was plenty of time to fight back, he didn't give the team any idea of how they might actually do it.

Oshie's impatience grew as he listened to the team talk. At last he could stand it no more.

"Mr Wilkes," he said. "Can I say something?"

"Go on, what is it?" said Mr Wilkes impatiently.

"They've got their slowest player at left-back and we're not testing him at all," said Oshie. "Our fastest man's Lewis and he's in the centre of the park. If we put him out on the right he'll skin that wing-back."

No one was sure what to say.

"What do you think, Lewis?" asked Mr Wilkes.

"I was thinking that," said Lewis.

"You've obviously got an eye for the game, Oshie," said Mr Wilkes.

"I've watched a lot of football," replied Oshie. With that, he hobbled round till he was facing the whole team. "Now I'll tell you what else we're doing wrong," he said.

"You're not the coach!" said Fred.

"No, let him speak," said Lewis, and others agreed.

Oshie's eyes were as sharp as glass. "We're too static," he said. "People are passing the ball, then just watching. We've got to give and go. Pass and move. Find the spaces, make ourselves available."

"I was thinking that," said Dylan.

"And as for you," said Oshie, "you want to spray the ball around like Beckham but you've got to *get* the thing first. You haven't put in a single tackle."

"I have!" said Dylan.

"No, you haven't, Dylan," said Jamie. "I'm doing all the work!"

"Yes, Jamie," said Oshie. "But you're also the reason they've scored three goals."

"Eh?" said Jamie.

"You keep playing them onside," said Oshie. "We've got to get the back line moving up together. Calum, you should be organizing it."

Calum didn't disagree. By now Oshie had

won everyone's respect. He knew what he was talking about.

"Maybe you should make Oshie coach, sir," suggested Lewis.

"I'm not sure I can do that," replied Mr Wilkes.

"Course you can do it, sir!" said Calum. "You're a teacher."

"You could be general manager," suggested Jamie.

Surprisingly, Mr Wilkes agreed. The truth was, he could see Adams Green getting stuffed, and the stick he'd take for it.

Full of new purpose, Adams Green went out for the second half. Just as Oshie had predicted, Lewis was soon running rings round Rushwood's left-back. Ten minutes into the half, he got to the byline and sent over a cross which Josh tapped back for Fred to lash into the net.

Now everyone's tails were up. For the next ten minutes all the pressure came from Adams Green Primary. Lewis got through again and put the ball into the penalty area, where a desperate defender sliced it into his own net.

The score was 2–3. Surely now Adams Green could come back to clinch it.

But would they? Rushwood regrouped, pulled their game together and began to dominate again. Out on the touchline, Oshie watched anxiously.

"Warm up, Jenna," he said.

"You're putting me on?" asked Jenna.

"We've got to get more ball," replied Oshie.

Two minutes later, Oshie held up the substitute board. Dylan Evans's number was on it.

Dylan's jaw dropped. No one substituted the Adams Green David Beckham!

But no, there was no mistake. Oshie beckoned Dylan off the pitch, clapped him on the back and sent on his secret weapon.

Jenna tore onto the pitch, fuelled by years of frustration. She set about the opposition like a buzzing bluebottle, the kind you swat and swat but can't get rid of. Almost every tackle ended with the ball at Jenna's feet. She passed it short, quick and simple, always finding her man, and soon the ammunition was being loaded down the right wing again. With the ball coming time and again into the Rushwood penalty area, the chances were sure to come. After a goal-mouth scramble, the Rushwood goalie palmed it straight to Fred, who bundled home his second goal.

Ten minutes left, and all to play for. Adams Green were starting to flag, but the sight of Oshie hobbling up and down the touchline, urging them on, spurred them into one last effort. Once again Lewis got the ball into the box. Josh got on the end of it and a Rushwood back took his leg. There was a loud blast on the ref's whistle. Penalty!

Only one problem. Dylan took the penalties. No one else wanted the responsibility.

"I'll take it," said Jenna.

The boys didn't argue. Jenna had already proved she had guts.

Everyone fell silent.

Jenna lined up the ball, took four confident steps back, then cracked it into the right-hand corner.

It was a good penalty. But the Rushwood goalie had read it. He flung himself to his left and beat the ball out. Quick as a flea, Jenna was onto it, and with a delicate flick, clipped the ball over the goalie and into the net.

Adams Green went into wild celebrations, but Oshie, focused as ever, ordered everyone back into position. The game wasn't over – not for a minute, anyway. Then, at last, the whistle blew on the greatest comeback in the Schools Cup history. Fred brimmed with the joy of victory – suddenly all his bad feelings about Oshie disappeared. The whole team lifted their new coach into the air and carried him around the pitch in triumph. For a short while, Oshie had twenty-two legs, and they all worked perfectly.

• • •

Long after everyone had gone, Jenna was still packing up her kit, savouring her triumph. As she set off for home she caught sight of Oshie, sitting on a bench outside the school gates. His eyes were red.

"Are you all right, Osh?" asked Jenna.

Oshie didn't reply, because he honestly didn't know why he'd been crying. Maybe it was for the footballing legs he'd never have, maybe it was because he was accepted now, maybe it was neither, or both. Either way, he felt better with Jenna there.

"Well done, Jenna," he said.

"Well done, Oshie," replied Jenna.

"See you tomorrow then," said Oshie.

"Can't avoid you, can I?" said Jenna.

Jenna kept a straight face, but Oshie saw the smile behind it. They went their separate ways, Oshie's right toes scraping their way home, Jenna suddenly aware of all the things in nature that ought to be perfect and weren't, but were beautiful all the same.

A Hippo on a Couch

Dylan Evans had a cultured left foot. That's what he called it. No one was sure what a cultured left foot was, but they were all sure he'd got one, because he could land a football on a pound coin from ten yards. He had an outswinger, an inswinger, a swivel kick and a banana. Dylan Evans didn't pass the ball, he caressed it. An invisible length of elastic connected it to his boot so that it never strayed to places he hadn't chosen. In short, Dylan Evans was a master and the ball was his slave.

As we know, Oshie saw everything and was quite aware of Dylan's cultured left foot. But there was a problem with Dylan. Dylan was a prima donna. Oshie told him so to his face. No one was sure what a prima donna was, but they were pretty sure Dylan was that as well.

There had been bad blood between Oshie and Dylan ever since the semi-final, when Dylan had been substituted. Dylan was convinced they'd have won by even more if he'd stayed on the pitch, and every practice afterwards was a chance to prove a point. After every defence-splitting pass and each immaculate shot, he'd turn his head towards Oshie and give a little smile, a smile without pleasure, a smile of challenge.

Little did he know it, but that challenge was about to be taken up, in a way Dylan could never have expected.

• • •

It was a Tuesday evening practice. As usual, Oshie had the squad doing fitness training for the first half-hour. While the others skipped, sprinted, star-jumped and squat-thrusted, Dylan dawdled round some cones, making faces at his mates.

"Come on, Dylan," said Oshie.

"I don't need fitness training," said Dylan.

"Why's that?" asked Oshie.

"'Cos I'm fit," said Dylan.

"You are not fit!" said Oshie. "You're a passenger for the last twenty minutes of every game!"

"How do you know?" countered Dylan. "You took me off for the last twenty minutes of the last one."

Everyone stopped. They sensed a fight brewing, but Oshie kept his cool. "It doesn't matter how skilled you are," he said. "If you can't run for sixty minutes you're not playing in the final."

Dylan was furious. Being substituted was bad enough. Starting on the bench – or maybe not even that – was the ultimate insult.

"What gets me about you," he said, "is that you expect us to do everything you say, but you *never* do what the teachers say. You're always messing about."

Oshie couldn't deny it.

"OK," said Oshie. "I know a way to prove

if you're fit enough. If you pass, you play. If you don't, you do fitness training."

"Go on," said Dylan. "What is it?"

"We have a race around the school field," replied Oshie.

"What – you and me?" scoffed Dylan, scarcely able to believe what he was hearing.

"Yeah, you and me," replied Oshie.

This really was ridiculous. Oshie could barely walk, let alone run. Maybe he supposed Dylan would be embarrassed to race a disabled person and just wouldn't try. Or maybe he thought Dylan would go racing off, then run out of puff so that Oshie could hobble past, like the tortoise and the hare. Either way, Oshie had made a big mistake.

"OK, you're on," said Dylan.

• • •

Jenna had heard the argument between Dylan and Oshie and was worried for her new friend. She knew Oshie was headstrong, and if he got in a conflict he hated to back down. He was constantly arguing back to teachers, which was why he spent every other dinner-time sitting outside the head's office. If he hadn't got those blue eyes and cheeky smile they'd have probably thrown him out by now. But his blue eyes and cheeky smile wouldn't help him in a race with Dylan Evans.

"What are you trying to do, Oshie?" she asked as they left school.

Oshie didn't reply.

"If you're thinking he'll back down, he won't," added Jenna.

Still Oshie didn't reply.

"Do you want to come round my house?" asked Jenna. "I've taken some videos on my new mobile and we can watch them on my telly."

"Can't," said Oshie. "I've got hippo therapy."

"Hippo therapy?" repeated Jenna.

"That's right," replied Oshie.

"What on earth is *hippo therapy*?" asked Jenna.

"What does it sound like?" asked Oshie.

"Like a hippo on a couch talking about its problems," replied Jenna.

"That's exactly what it is," said Oshie.

"Must be a strong couch," quipped Jenna.

"It is," replied Oshie.

"Aren't hippos dangerous?" asked Jenna.

"Only if they don't get therapy," replied Oshie.

Jenna nodded thoughtfully. She knew it was all rubbish, but she often had these kinds of conversations with Oshie. It was an unwritten rule that you pretended to take them seriously.

"Are you *sure* you know what you're doing?" pressed Jenna.

"Probably not," replied Oshie.

Probably not confirmed Jenna's worst fears. Oshie had bitten off more than he could chew. She repeated what he had said to her best friend, Emma, and soon the word spread that Oshie knew he wouldn't really win. Fred was taking bets on the race, and already the fifty ps were flying in for Dylan, while not a penny was laid on Oshie. Fred made Dylan ten-to-one on favourite, which meant that you only got one pence back for every ten you put on. Oshie went out to fifty-to-one against, but even that price didn't tempt anyone.

That all changed on Thursday lunchtime, the day before the race was due to take place. Most of the team were kicking a flat ball around the playground when an excited Fred stopped the game. "I've just taken a bet on Oshie," he said.

"Never!" said Dylan.

"How much?" asked Josh.

"Ten quid," replied Fred.

"Ten quid?" gasped Josh. "Who's put ten quid on?"

"A boy from year four," replied Fred. "But it wasn't his money."

"Whose money was it?" asked Dylan.

"He wouldn't say," replied Fred.

"Probably Oshie's," said Josh.

"I thought he didn't think he could win," said Dylan.

"He better not," said Fred. "I'll be down five hundred nicker!"

Dylan went very quiet. For all his big talk, he still had doubts about this race. Was it possible that Oshie wasn't really as disabled as he pretended? After all, it was a great way of getting out of PE and all those running jobs teachers gave you. And look how the girls flocked around him, fussed over him and offered to carry his bag.

As soon as Dylan thought these thoughts, he began to believe them. He tested them out on a couple of his friends, in a half-joking way, to see how they reacted. Lewis was having none of it, but Calum said he'd been thinking the same thing. Maybe Oshie did have *something* wrong with him, but it wasn't as bad as he made out.

Soon the new rumour spread around school, and when Jenna heard it she was furious. How could the boys be so stupid as to think Oshie was faking! Hadn't they seen him out of school? Did they think he was still acting when he didn't know anyone was watching him?

Then a thought struck Jenna. Most of the boys didn't see Oshie out of school. He lived on the far side of the estate, well away from their houses. In fact, Jenna didn't see Oshie that often, and when she did, he was always expecting her.

Jenna knew that Oshie went shopping with his grandma on Thursday evenings. If she waited near Lidl with her new mobile phone, she could video him and prove to everybody, including herself, how genuine he was.

• • •

That evening, Jenna lay in wait behind the bushes at the side of the Lidl car park. She felt bad about doing this, but it would all be for the best. She knew roughly what time Oshie would be there – he was almost certainly in the shop already. But if so, he was taking an age to come out.

Suddenly, up ahead, she caught sight of two figures. They were coming towards her from the far end of the road. One was on a bike and the other was running alongside. As they drew closer the figures became familiar. The one on the bike, who held a stopwatch in one hand, was Fred. The one running, puffing and blowing, with a bright red face, was Dylan.

"Come on, Dylan!" urged Fred. "Push it!"

"Need a break!" gasped Dylan.

So saying, Dylan ground to a halt, bent over double and heaved for breath. By now they were only a few metres from Jenna. She came out from her hidey-hole with her mobile in her hand.

"Hi, guys," she said. "Check yourselves out on YouTube later."

"Jenna!" gasped Dylan. "You'd better not!"

"Good to see you getting fit, Dyl," said Jenna.

"I'm already fit!" panted Dylan.

At that moment two more figures came into view by the supermarket. Oshie's gran was struggling along with about four bags of shopping. Beside her, Oshie leant on his gran's shopping wheels, struggling to push them forward.

Thankfully, there would be no need for video evidence.

A knot of pupils, mainly boys, some girls, waited on the school field at five to four the next day. Dylan was posing, doing a few stretching exercises. Though he tried to look cool, he checked his watch every few seconds and cast anxious glances around the field. It was a big field, one of the largest in the county, and last night's run had made his chest sore and his muscles ache. Dylan really wasn't fit, and even if he beat Oshie by a mile, he'd still look stupid if he had to stop halfway round to catch his breath.

But for that to happen there'd have to be a race, and there was still no sign of Oshie. Already a rumour was going round that he'd bottled it, and as the seconds ticked towards four, that rumour was becoming more and more convincing.

Then, just as Dylan was about to declare a walkover, there was an excited shout: "He's here!"

The pupils turned as one towards the school gate. There, an astonishing sight met their eyes. Oshie had indeed arrived, but he was not alone. Oshie sat like a little prince, high in the air, riding the most beautiful chestnut pony. With a cheerful wave, Oshie trotted onto the field as cool and easy as a cowboy moseying up a trail.

"You can't race me on that!" cried Dylan.

"Why not?" asked Oshie.

"We're racing on foot!" protested Dylan.

"Who said that?" asked Oshie.

Dylan wheeled about, looking for support, but all the boys except Fred were laughing and the girls were going gooey at the pony.

"Tell you what," said Oshie. "I'll give you fifty metres' start."

"I'm not racing a horse!" cried Dylan.

"Pony," corrected Oshie.

Again Dylan looked for support, but all that met him were eager eyes, hungry to see this piece of entertainment.

"OK," said Oshie. "I'll make it really easy for you. I'll let you get halfway round the field before I start."

Dylan checked out the field again. Halfway round was a long way. If he jogged the first half really easy, then went like the clappers...

"Fred," he said. "You make sure he doesn't go before he's supposed to."

Dylan knew he could rely on Fred. Fred still stood to lose a lot of money if Dylan didn't win.

Fred announced that he was the starter. He stood in front of Oshie's pony and brought down his hand. Dylan jogged off at a snail's pace, to jeers from the crowd. Eventually he was no more than a speck in the distance, at which point Fred finally gave the go-ahead to Oshie. Oshie set off at a casual canter, totally at ease, seemingly unaware he was in a race.

Dylan glanced over. Suddenly he was off like a rat up a drainpipe. Not many people had seen Dylan run before, and certainly not that fast. It really was impressive for the first twenty metres or so. Then his legs began to slow, his head began to nod and his lead over Oshie began to shrink. With about a hundred metres to go, Oshie was almost upon him, and Dylan's sprint had become no more than a breathless stagger. Rather than gallop past, however, Oshie slowed his pony to a trot, settling just behind his rival.

By now the crowd were in stitches, watching the great prima donna panting like a red-faced clown, desperate for the finish line. Just as Dylan began to believe he might make it, however, Oshie eased his pony onto the outside and gently clip-clopped past, arriving back where they began to a huge cheer.

"Don't worry, Fred," were his first words. "I don't want the money." With just a little difficulty he dismounted and held out his hand to the wheezing figure behind.

Dylan hardly had the strength to shake it.

"Good effort, Dyl," said Oshie. "Fitness practice starts at three-thirty Monday."

Long after everyone had gone, Jenna and Oshie were still laughing about the day's events.

"You kept that pony a secret," said Jenna.

"I told you I did hippotherapy," replied Oshie.

"Hippotherapy is riding a horse?" asked Jenna.

"She helps me walk better," said Oshie. "Don't you, Mizzi?"

Jenna's face had suddenly become glum.

"What's the matter?" asked Oshie.

"I liked the idea of a hippo on a couch," replied Jenna.

Oshie patted his pony's head, smiling broadly.

Lakes of Death

On the weekend before the big game, there was a knock on Jenna's door. It was Oshie. His eyes were full of mischief.

"You doing anything?" he asked.

"You're not going to make me train on a Saturday!" groaned Jenna.

"Nah, I'm bored of football," said Oshie. "Want to come on a hunt?"

"A fox hunt?" asked Jenna.

"A rare bird hunt," replied Oshie.

This was a surprise to Jenna. She didn't

know Oshie was interested in birds. "Are you going to kill it?" she asked.

"No, just take a picture," replied Oshie.

"What kind of bird is it?" asked Jenna.

"A bittern," replied Oshie.

"A bitten?" said Jenna.

"Bit*tern*," corrected Oshie.

"I don't know anything about birds," confessed Jenna.

"A bittern's a big wading bird," explained Oshie. "Very shy."

"So how will we find one?" asked Jenna.

"There's one at Doverton Lakes," said Oshie. "I read it on a website."

The mention of Doverton Lakes scared Jenna. "Children have drowned there," she told Oshie.

"We're not going to swim to find it!" he scoffed.

"Let's go shopping," suggested Jenna.

Oshie groaned.

"We could hunt for bargains," said Jenna, hopefully.

"Let's draw cards," said Oshie. "If I win, we hunt the bittern. If you win, we hunt bargains."

Jenna fetched a pack of cards and drew out the queen of diamonds. After considering for a short while, Oshie drew his own card. It was the ace of spades.

"I win!" he cried.

"That's the death card!" said Jenna.

"Pah!" scoffed Oshie. "Stupid superstition!"

Jenna was not so sure.

The light was strange at Doverton Lakes. There was a bright sun, but it shone beneath a dark blanket of cloud, like a torch under a duvet. Oshie's eyes looked bluer than ever in this light, almost unreal.

"Give some bread to the birds," suggested Oshie, handing a crust to Jenna.

Jenna threw the bread towards a crowd of swans at the lake's edge. In seconds she was drowning in a sea of hungry beaks, before her, beside her, behind her, all pecking

furiously. Jenna covered her head and screamed. Oshie couldn't stop laughing.

"That wasn't funny!" cried Jenna.

"Your face!" said Oshie.

"I hate geese!" said Jenna.

"They're swans," said Oshie. "Don't you know any birds?"

"I know a hammafor," said Jenna.

"What's a hammafor?" asked Oshie.

"Knocking nails in," said Jenna.

Now they were even.

• • •

There was a boardwalk around the lakes, through a forest of high feathery rushes which pecked in the breeze. Jenna liked the feeling of the springy wood beneath her feet and the sense of being lost, but not really lost, in a picture-book world. Everything was fun with Oshie. Those lively eyes missed nothing. Oshie reeled off the names of the birds he spotted, the reed buntings and the sedge warblers, the water rails and the long-tailed tits. They all sounded exotic and exciting, much more exciting than the plain old bittern. But it was the bittern that obsessed Oshie, and the bittern was nowhere to be seen.

"What does a bittern look like?" asked Jenna.

"Like a heron," explained Oshie, "only squatter and browner."

"What does a heron look like?" asked Jenna.

"Like a bittern," replied Oshie, "only thinner and greyer."

"How would you like to look like Oshie," said Jenna, "only with a big red slap-mark on your cheek?"

Oshie's face fell. "Don't say that," he murmured.

Jenna suddenly felt terrible. "I didn't mean it," she said.

For a moment Oshie seemed on the verge of tears. Then, like lightning, his right hand shot out and playfully cuffed Jenna round her own cheek.

"I'll kill you!" she shouted.

Oshie fled, but of course he couldn't go very fast, and Jenna caught him just around the corner, where a new length of boardwalk stretched off into the far distance. Jenna pretended to be crushing Oshie to death, but it was really an excuse to be close.

Suddenly Oshie looked up. A tiny figure, far off down the boardwalk, was jumping and waving and calling his name. Oshie's face lit up.

"Ella!" he cried.

The tiny figure ran full pelt towards them, arms wide like a plane, as Oshie's grin broke into a chuckle of delight.

"It's my cousin!" he explained.

Oshie broke away from Jenna and held out his own arms.

"Yobby-yobby-yobby!" he yelled.

"Yobby-yobby-yobby!" came the reply. Oshie's cousin was in clear view now. She was a stunning-looking girl, with a wide curvy mouth, dark liquid eyes, caramel skin and a black mane of hair streaming in the wind. As she approached she began to laugh, then crashed into Oshie, sending him spinning like a signpost in a gale. It was a miracle they didn't topple off the boardwalk.

"Is Kali here?" asked Oshie, eagerly.

"She's with Grandma," replied Ella. "What are you doing?"

"Hunting a bittern," replied Oshie.

"Can I come?" asked Ella.

"Yeah, come along!" said Oshie.

Jenna's spirits sank. Oshie introduced them, but Ella was busy ringing her mum.

Jenna didn't even bother with a hello.

Oshie and Ella certainly had a lot to talk about. Friends, cousins, parties they'd been to, films they'd watched, clothes they'd bought ... a whole world of things they had in common, a world which didn't seem to include football, but most certainly included birds. Ella was as excited as Oshie about hunting a bittern, and could even imitate the bittern's distinctive booming call, a call they would not hear today, because, of course, it was the wrong time of year.

Jenna didn't know it was the wrong time of year to hear the bittern's boom. But she did know it was the wrong time of year to bump into Ella.

"I saw something!" Jenna suddenly said. She hadn't, but she did get Oshie's attention at last.

"What did it look like?" asked Oshie.

"Brown," said Jenna.

Oshie looked about.
They'd come off the boardwalk
and were on a muddy path through
a thicket of trees, away from the lake.

"The bittern won't be here," said Ella.

"I know that," replied Jenna.

"What do you think it was then?" asked Ella.

At that moment, Jenna happened to catch sight of a small bird hopping about in the undergrowth, a bird that looked very familiar, so familiar that even she knew its name.

"Oh," she said. "It's only a sparrow."

Ella followed Jenna's gaze. A look of disbelief came over her. "That's not a sparrow!" she laughed. "That's a dunnock!"

Jenna felt her face flush. She wanted to walk quickly on and forget her stupid mistake, but Ella wasn't done yet. "Whoever heard of a sparrow with a grey head?" she trilled.

"Whoever heard of a sparrow with a grey head?" mimicked Jenna. It came out before she could stop herself.

"Don't laugh at me," said Ella.

"Don't laugh at me then," said Jenna.

The two girls glared at each other. What a cow, thought Jenna. How could Oshie like her so much? Maybe Oshie didn't deserve to be Jenna's friend.

"I'm going to find that bird on my own," declared Jenna. "You better hope you find it before me, because when I find it, I'm going to kill it."

The blanket of cloud had blotted out the sun by the time Oshie and Ella reached the last of the Doverton lakes. This was a desolate place where you could still tell that the area had once been a limestone quarry. Patches of it were like a desert, only a few scrawny bushes growing on the slithery grey earth. But there were still reed-beds, and just maybe a bittern lurking within them.

There had been no sign of Jenna since the argument. Oshie and Ella had laughed it off at first, but now the fun and laughter had ended and Ella had fallen into a sullen silence. Oshie still pointed out the cormorants, the grebes and the tufted ducks, but inside he was growing anxious.

Oshie and Ella reached the far end of the lake. Here was a grassy bank which sloped gently down to the water, providing a view over to a reed-bed which couldn't be reached by any path. Something was on that bank, down near the water. At first it looked like a bird or a small animal, but as they drew closer they realized it was no such thing. It was a pair of trainers.

Oshie's anxiety grew. The lake at this point was fringed by a shallow shelf, giving the impression you could paddle out safely towards the reed-bed. But that would be a terrible mistake. Just beyond that shallow water was the edge of the old quarry, a sudden headlong drop to unspeakable depths.

Ella and Oshie reached the trainers. With a thumping heart, Oshie now knew what he had feared most.

"They're Jenna's trainers," he said.

"You don't think she'd have gone in the water?" asked Ella.

"Get the warden!" cried Oshie.

Ella fled back towards the entrance to the country park, arms and legs a flurry of panic. Oshie followed as fast as he was able, falling over twice in his urgency.

Meanwhile, in a nearby thicket, two still, silent eyes watched his every move.

Only when Oshie had gone did the silent watcher come out of hiding.

Jenna knew that she'd done a terrible thing. For a moment she considered fleeing, leaving the country, or even going in that water for real. Of course, she had wanted them to find the trainers, wanted them to think she had drowned, but to see them run like that, to see Oshie's struggle to save her...

Now Jenna ran. She ran with every ounce of strength in her body. Her trainers were in her hand and her feet were cut and bruised by the path of limestone spoil. There was no chance of catching Ella, but Oshie was soon in view, limping and stumbling with desperate effort.

Jenna yelled Oshie's name. He stopped and turned. Jenna hobbled to meet him, holding the shoes aloft.

"Lost me trainers!" she cried.

Oshie had a face of stone. "What did you do that for?" he snapped.

"What?" said Jenna.

Oshie rang Ella on his mobile and told her that Jenna was OK. She'd just been playing a stupid practical joke.

"It wasn't a joke," said Jenna.

"What was it then?" demanded Oshie.

Jenna felt a cry coming, but Jenna wasn't a girl who cried. She choked it back, but when she spoke, her voice trembled. "You asked me here today," she said. "I never agreed to meet your cousin. Why did you just ignore me and talk to her all the time, like I was too stupid to talk to?"

"I see you every day," replied Oshie. "I see her once a month."

"That's no excuse to ignore me!" cried Jenna.

"I wasn't ignoring you on purpose," replied Oshie.

"I don't know if you even like me!" cried Jenna.

"Course I like you!" replied Oshie. "You wouldn't be my best friend if I didn't like you!"

"Am I?" asked Jenna.

"Course you are!" replied Oshie.

Jenna suddenly felt stupider than ever. Of course Oshie liked her! And of course Ella wasn't a cow. Ella had tried to save her life.

Jenna hated to say sorry, but she was practising the word in her head when she saw that Oshie's expression had changed. His eyes were alert, focused and deadly serious.

"Don't move," he said.

Steadily, like a creeping cat, Oshie lifted his camera strap over his head,

opened the case, and held the camera up towards Jenna. Suddenly self-conscious, Jenna turned her head. She heard the click of the shutter, one, two, three times. Then, mercifully, it was over.

"Why did you take that picture?" asked Jenna, much later, when they were home.

Oshie smiled. He took out his camera, clicked it onto "view" and held it to

Jenna's eyes. There, in the little square viewer, were two round eyes, a long pointed beak and a mottled-brown body, almost completely camouflaged amongst the reeds.

"I'll always remember this day," said Oshie.

"So will I," said Jenna.

The Loose Cannon

Oshie's days as the new boy came to an end with the arrival of Liam Grist. In many people's eyes, Liam was not only new to school, but also to Planet Earth. He wore his hair gelled up into a crest and had his own take on school uniform, with a turned up collar and a pair of short, baggy trousers which looked like they'd been cut down from his dad's. Liam Grist held his mouth permanently open as if amazed by everything he saw, saw through eyes as pale as water, eyes with a glint of madness.

Liam Grist was not very bright. He struggled to write or understand the simplest sums. For some reason Oshie took it upon himself to help the new boy with his basic skills, and the two of them quickly formed a bond. And it really was a bond, as Liam liked to hook his arm around Oshie's and tell everyone he was Liam's best mate, a really great guy, and almost as good-looking as Liam.

Oshie was not too comfortable with being hugged so often and so tightly, but for some reason he put up with it. Maybe he sensed that Liam would be brilliant at football.

And brilliant Liam was. The moment he first picked up a ball at practice, played keepy-uppy for five minutes, then flicked it onto the back of his neck, it was obvious he had skill.

He could dribble like a monkey, twist and pivot on a sixpence, feint, lob and flick like George Best.

But just as important, he played with such fire and energy it was as if everyone else was standing still – which some were, just to watch the entertainment.

After twenty minutes of Liam's first practice, Oshie was already pencilling him in for the big game. Then Liam went for a fifty-fifty ball with Jamie, and Jamie met him with a shoulder barge. It was a fair barge, perfectly legal, but Liam was off-balance and as a result went flying through the air and landed flat-out in the mud. That brought a few sniggers from the boys who were jealous of the new boy's skill. It also brought a change in Liam. The smile left his face and was replaced by a deadly frown. For the next five minutes he hunted Jamie up and down the pitch relentlessly. Then, when the chance came, he mowed him down like a samurai.

The tackle left Jamie writhing in agony and everyone else crying out in protest. But Liam simply stood over his opponent, jeering that he'd got what he'd deserved, shame he couldn't take it.

After the practice Jenna walked home with Oshie. "You're not going to play him after that, are you?" she asked.

Oshie was strangely quiet.

"He's a nutter, Oshie!" continued Jenna.

"He's a genius," said Oshie, as if that was the last word on the matter.

Liam danced into school next day and presented Jamie with a bar of chocolate. "No hard feelings, mate," he said. The choccy bar had a piece missing, and Liam apologized for that as well. Then he gave Jamie a fat kiss on the forehead, which embarrassed Jamie so much he was rubbing the spot all morning.

Truth was, Oshie had had a word with Liam and told him that if he wanted to play for the team he'd have to cool it. And Liam did want to play for the team. He may have been new at Adams Green Primary but he knew all about the Schools Cup, and he badly wanted a piece of it.

The apology to Jamie convinced Oshie he could handle Liam, but others weren't so sure. With the big game just days away, trusting this new kid was a major risk.

Next day Liam brought a toy into school – a Transformer. He spent half the morning converting it from a robot to a truck and back again, till Mr Roberts caught sight of it under Liam's desk and demanded he hand it over.

Liam had no intention of handing the Transformer over. It belonged to him, not Mr Roberts. There was a tense face-off between them, then Mr Roberts swiped the toy from Liam's hands.

Liam went crazy. He took a wild swing at Mr Roberts, who immediately frogmarched him out of the classroom towards the head's office. As the class rushed to the door to see the action, Liam wrenched himself free and ran into the first room he saw, which happened to be the staffroom. What happened next was a mystery, but there was all kinds of shouting and uproar and teachers hurrying out with urgent faces. The class were ordered back into their room. Ten minutes passed, then an ambulance arrived in the playground.

When Liam returned to school the next day, there were bandages all over his left hand. "Don't need a hand to kick a football," he said to Oshie.

"You're never going to pick him now," said Jenna that lunchtime.

"Leave it, Jenna," replied Oshie. "He's playing."

"Why?" pleaded Jenna.

"It's a big game," replied Oshie. "Big games need big players."

"Not big idiots," countered Jenna.

"Look at the World Cup," said Oshie. "The team with the Maradona or the Zidane always wins. Everyone else is scared of the big stage, but the big players live for it."

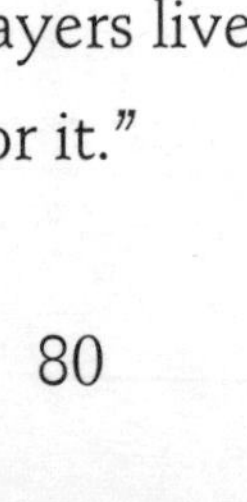

"Zidane got sent off in his last World Cup," replied Jenna. "He lost it."

Oshie had forgotten that. When it came to footy knowledge, Jenna was a match for anyone.

"Listen," he said. "It's my choice, and I'll take the flak if it goes wrong."

The team sheet went up that Thursday, the day before the final. Needless to say, Liam's name was the main talking point. Almost everyone agreed with Jenna that it was a gamble too far – none more than Kabir, who'd lost his place so Liam could play. Kabir was so mad he said he wouldn't be a sub, which got him a good telling-off from Mr Wilkes. Later in the day, however, Mr Wilkes took Oshie to one side and expressed his own concerns about Liam. It all added up to a lot of pressure on Oshie, but this only seemed to make him more determined.

• • •

Next day, when the minibus drew up to take the team to the game, the team sheet was exactly the same. Liam was first on the bus, buzzing with excitement. Just as Oshie had predicted, he was up for the big game, while everyone else seemed to be dreading it. Everyone except Kabir. Kabir wasn't there.

"Anyone seen Kabir?" asked Oshie.

"He ain't coming," replied Fred.

Oshie's spirits sank. That was the last thing he needed for team morale: a sub's bench one short because someone had had a strop. But he put a brave face on it.

"Looks like I'm playing!" he joked. Everyone laughed, and for a moment the tension was broken, then everybody except Liam sank back into fearful silence.

The cup final was being played at the county sports arena, a place most of the team had never even been to. As the Adams Green team pulled up in front of the smoked-glass space-station-like main entrance, the Broomsgrove team were already unloading from their own minibus. The minibus had Broomsgrove 1st XI painted on the side, and every player had an identical kitbag. It was as if they were one-up already.

"What a bunch of posers!" said Liam. His arm flashed up to make a gesture, but quick as a flash Oshie held it down. Mr Wilkes wagged a warning finger in Liam's direction. Mr Wilkes looked more nervous than the team, but about what it wasn't clear.

• • •

And so the game began, on a perfect pitch, in front of real stands, with real VIPs watching and the precious Schools Cup glinting in the sunshine. Broomsgrove started full of confidence, stroking the ball around, hardly giving Adams Green a look-in. There was an air of panic every time the ball got near the Adams Green penalty area, with even the most skilful players hoofing the ball away like total beginners. Oshie shouted himself hoarse on the touchline, urging everyone to calm down and remember the gameplan, but it made little difference: Adams Green had let the occasion get to them.

Then, at last, the ball came to Liam. He beat two men in an instant and raced off up the left touchline, waving the rest of the team forward with a frantic arm. Then he cut back suddenly, losing another two opponents, and laid a perfect ball in Lewis's path, only to see Lewis shank it halfway to the corner flag. But Broomsgrove's spell was broken. Now it was their players who showed doubts on the ball and Adams Green who grew in confidence. Over on the touchline a small smile of satisfaction crept onto Oshie's face.

The smile didn't last long. Liam was tripped by a Broomsgrove midfielder but the referee waved to play on. Liam pursued the ref halfway down the pitch, raging and swearing and calling him blind. The referee stopped play, reached into his pocket, and pulled out a yellow card. Everyone except Liam knew that he was lucky not to see red.

Half-time arrived with the game still goalless. Oshie was all set for his team talk, but Liam was still raging about the ref, and in the end Mr Wilkes had to step in to stop a blazing row between Liam and the rest of the team. Some were openly saying Liam should be subbed, but Jamie had turned his ankle and one of Adams Green's two remaining subs was already set to go on. It was a gamble to carry on with Liam, but, to Oshie's mind, an even bigger gamble to use up the last sub.

Oshie settled on a quiet word in Liam's ear.

"Just cool it, Liam," he said.

"I'm cool, I'm cool," replied Liam, but his eyes told a different story.

Broomsgrove had changed their tactics in the second half. They'd decided to man-mark Liam. As soon as Oshie saw this, he called to Liam to rove all over the park, and Jenna to push forward into the gaps in midfield. Adams Green soon began to get on top of Broomsgrove, making raid after raid, but they all broke down at Broomsgrove's solid central defenders. One of these raids ended up with Josh streaming blood after a clash of heads: on came Leon, Adams Green's last remaining sub.

Then Adams Green got a break. A Broomsgrove defender cleared the ball straight into the back of a team-mate. The ball fell to Liam, who broke like a rocket, angled a perfect pass to Lewis on the wing, then sprinted into the penalty box, screaming for a return ball.

This time Lewis put the ball exactly in the right place. All Liam needed to do was meet it with a sidefoot to the left of the goalie. The net bulged, the crowd roared, Liam punched the sky, kissed his school crest, then proceeded to rip off his shirt.

Some people think it's a stupid law to book a player for taking off their shirt. Nevertheless, it is a law, and refs are duty-bound to uphold it. To the horror of Liam's team-mates, the ref did exactly that, pulling out a yellow swiftly followed by a red.

Needless to say, Liam did not go quietly. In fact, if Fred, Oshie and Mr Wilkes had not all intervened, Liam might well have got the game abandoned and handed to Broomsgrove. As Liam sloped off the pitch, however, the damage was serious enough. With ten men, and no Liam, Adams Green were on a hiding to nothing.

Back on the touchline, Oshie watched the game unfold with a heavy heart. His team were under the hammer, his gamble had backfired, and as he'd said to Jenna, all the blame would lie with him if Adams Green lost.

But they hadn't lost yet. By some miracle and half a dozen goal-mouth scrambles, Oshie's team held on. Then Calum went in for a tackle and came out with an agonizing dead-leg. He limped around for a minute or two but the situation was hopeless. Calum came off and the team were down to nine men.

Jenna looked out to the touchline for new instructions from Oshie. Her friend was nowhere to be seen.

A hundred thoughts flashed through Jenna's mind and they were all bad. A terrible feeling of emptiness came over her, a feeling which made her want to give up and walk off the pitch. But of course, Jenna, was a fighter. She put the bad thoughts behind her and threw herself back into the fray, running and tackling like a demon, until it seemed as if Adams Green had two men extra, not two less. Somehow, amazingly, Adams Green hung on to their lead as the clock ticked down.

But Broomsgrove had the scent of victory in their nostrils. All they needed was one goal to force extra time. Against nine tired players the rest would be easy.

With just two minutes left, Broomsgrove got the chance they'd been waiting for. Fred made a poor back pass, which was intercepted by the Broomsgrove winger, who sped past Leon and squared it to Broomsgrove's big blond forward. With one quick sidestep he was past Jenna and into the penalty area. As Jake advanced from his goal, the forward drew back his foot and cracked an absolute cannonball. The ball flew past Jake, on a certain course for the top corner, when somehow, from nowhere, a defender's head got in its way. The defender ended up flat on the ground, possibly unconscious, while the ball flew back past the attacker to be heaved to safety by a grateful Fred. As the full-time whistle blew, the brave defender pulled himself up onto his knees, revealing an unmistakable pair of blue eyes, just below a wicked red mark the shape of half a football.

"Oshie!" cried Jenna.

Oshie was besieged by his team yanking him to his feet with wild roars of celebration.

Before, he'd just been a good coach. Now he was a legend.

Early that evening, Jenna and Oshie sat on the wasteland near Jenna's house, watching the sun set. The wind had turned cold, but there was a warm feeling inside them.

"When did you decide to be a sub?" asked Jenna.

"When I said I would," replied Oshie.

"Everyone thought it was a joke," said Jenna.

"So did I, till I'd said it," replied Oshie.

Jenna threw a pebble at the stick they'd set up. It was a satisfying direct hit, catapulting the stick out of the ground.

"One–nil!" she cried, then laughed.

Oshie groaned. "Now we're going to have to play till I'm in front," he said.

"We'll be here all night," joked Jenna.

"I really don't think so, Jenna," replied Oshie.

Oshie reset the stick, concentrated hard, then cracked the next pebble right on top of it. "One–all!" he cried.

"Don't be so competitive," said Jenna, and they exchanged one of their secret smiles, a smile that said they knew exactly what the other was thinking, a smile that promised they would be sparring for many years to come, possibly for ever.

A note from the author:

The inspiration for Oshie was my own son, Jordi, who was diagnosed with cerebral palsy around the age of two. It occurred to me that there were few, if any, heroes of children's fiction with CP, so I began conceiving the Oshie stories, imagining Jordi as a ten- or eleven-year-old. While the stories obviously deal with disability, it was important to me that they were not all about disability – it is Oshie's character which is central. While I'm always aware of Jordi's difficulties with movement, he is fantastically enthusiastic, clever and funny, not to mention wilful and contrary. I strove to make Oshie similarly engaging, and his friendship with Jenna one to which many children could relate.

I can't remember why I decided to write the book about football. When I was young I was always kicking a ball about, and it's sad that Jordi can't do the same. But I strongly believe that any disadavantage can be turned into an advantage, and hopefully the stories in Oshie demonstrate this.

Cerebral palsy is the most common cause of disability, affecting about one in 400 people. Caused by damage to the brain before, during or after birth, it may be mild enough to be almost unnoticeable, or severe enough to to make any movement, including speech, extremely difficult. Oshie's disability is relatively mild: the book doesn't pretend to speak for all those with CP.

CP is incurable but its effects can be lessened by various means, particularly physiotherapy. The NHS provides basic help, but at present it is still down to a charity, the Bobath Institute (**www.bobath.org.uk**), to provide more in-depth physio. They do fantastic work.

There is too much emphasis in our society on being physically perfect, as if this is somehow normal. I'm very aware of this, not just because of Jordi, but also because I used to be slim and athletic and now I'm definitely not. I haven't become a worse person because of it.

Jon Blake is the author of over fifty books for children and teenagers. He was brought up in Southampton and now lives in Cardiff. Jon's successes include *You're a Hero, Daley B*; *Little Stupendo*; *One Girl School* and the House of Fun series. He is noted for his humour, but as *Oshie* shows, his writing has a serious side too.

Anuska Allepuz was born in 1979 in Madrid. After studying Fine Art at the University of Salamanca, she lived in Berlin and did illustration work with several charity organizations. Anuska completed a postgraduate illustration course in Barcelona, and her work was exhibited at the Bologna Children's Bookfair in 2009, as well as other exhibitions. Anuska currently lives in London.